T0197652

ADVENTURES OF CAPTAIN ZERO

CHAPTER 2

BABAK NADERI

Order this book online at www.trafford.com
or email orders@trafford.com

Most Trafford titles are also available at major online book retailers.

Trafford PUBLISHING® www.trafford.com

North America & international
toll-free: 844 688 6899 (USA & Canada)
fax: 812 355 4082

Our mission is to efficiently provide the world's finest, most comprehensive book publishing service, enabling every author to experience success. To find out how to publish your book, your way, and have it available worldwide, visit us online at www.trafford.com

ISBN: 978-1-6987-0570-5 (sc)

ISBN: 978-1-6987-0571-2 (e)

Print information available on the last page.

Trafford rev. 01/29/2021

"ADVENTURES OF CAPTAIN ZERO CHAPTER 2"

By

Mr. Babak Naderi

"In honor & duty of King Mohammad Reza Shah Pahlavi"

Spring 2003. I had a vision that all the peaceful white men of England and all the white peaceful men of Iran stood up for me, all at once. Because the United States government wanted me dead. And then the Persian blue man went back to Iran and he drew a blue line in the middle of Iran from the west to the eastern border of Iran. And the blue man kept traveling on the train from east of Iran to the western border of Iran on the train along the way of the blue line seperating the northern Iran from the southern Persian Gulf of Iran. Then all the northern white peaceful women and men of Iran became angry and red. And all the white peaceful men of southern Iran turned green with envy and jealousy and then the blue man kept going from western Iran to the eastern Iran and he kept seperating the red north from the green south of Iran; until the seperating blue line became white and peaceful and that is when the train which the blue man of Iran was traveling on, the train stopped. And the blue line became a white line. And then the northern women of Iran were angry at the green jealous and envious men of the southern Persian Gulf of Iran.

By the end of 2010, I decided to move to Las Vegas, Nevada, USA. Four months later, I settled down in Las Vegas, Nevada, USA during the end of the world according to the Mayan calender and the Jewish calender year of 2011 A.D., suddenly it all happened at once, five UFOs landed on the northern coast of the Caspian Sea shaped like a Mongolian war lord's hat of their warrior men. Then two more UFOs landed on the Aztec, Mayan temple. One of the UFO was on one Mayan temple with its suction cup trying to pick up a Mayan baby. And my Spanish ex-girlfriend and a white man kept on giving one baby after another baby from the Spanish woman's womb and the white man kept on running up and down the Mayan temple and the UFO kept rejecting one offered baby after another offered baby and the UFO would not take any of the babies and the white man gave up all his efforts and he gave up all of his might and he became devastated and he ended up sitting on the very steps of the Mayan temple.

Meanwhile on top of the second Mayan temple, the second UFO was looking for a seperate Mayan Aztec baby. But a different white man kept running up and down the Mayan temple like a running man, but instead of feeding the second UFO suction cup a baby; this white man kept stuffing the UFO suction cup one assault rifle after another handgun and ammunitions and more weapons of destruction and the UFO kept on spitting the weapons out and the bullets kept on exploding on and about the other white man's legs and his feet and the UFO kept rejecting the manmade weapons and machine guns and bullets. Because, the UFO was looking for an Aztec, Mayan baby.

By the spring of 2011, while I was in Las Vegas, Nevada and while I was perceiving the two UFOs at the Mayan temple the other 5 UFOs took off early from the northern Caspian Sea Coast in Russia and those 5 UFOs are headed for the golden "Nero" end of our universe, which is below our dirt earth and this "Nero" end of our universe is expanded by 99999 light years and after the five UFOs exit the dirt earth's atmosphere, they must go thru a very rough tumultuous rocky, bumpy, impenetrable passage of the cosmos before the 5 UFOs get close enough to the black hole. This enormous black hole is suspended and blown out of the "Nero" end of the universe by the giant golden saxophone shaped, golden end of the "Nero" universe at the year 99999 light years away. And it is on this giant saxophone middle part where the "Allah" golden ship resides, just as it is written in Arabic, the ship "Allah" is made out of gold and it looks like the sailings of a manmade wooden ships of the British Empire. And combonation of the "Nero" end of our golden universe and its extended saxophoned and trumpeted golden outlet and the "Allah" golden spaceship residing like the manmade musical instrument finger pressed, valves, and the golden hatted golden spaceship of king of Persia, which covers and silences the golden trumpeted saxophoned extended end of our universe; before the black hole begins to be suspended outward and a bit off and away from the giant golden megaphoned end of our universe at the year of 99999 light years away. From the other end of our universe at the year 88888 light years away from each end to end.

And then by the winter of 2016 in Las Vegas, Nevada I envisioned a massive green tree landing from the green vegetation planet and on this green vegetative planet, there exists a giant holli molli, monni, mooii cow which keeps on getting bigger and bigger and this holli, molli, monni, mooii cow does not even drop a drop of milk. This green planet is located on the left side of the Zionist center of our universe, and this green tree has landed in New Delhi, India area by the time of winter 2011. And then by the beginning of winter of 2016, this green tree became detached from somewhere in New Delhi, India Hidustan and this green tree has retracted back to the green planet and then immediately this green tree restarted to grow and twist back towards dirt earth from the green vegetated planet. And this, long twisted green tree with leaves has landed again, but this time by winter of 2016, it has landed in Buffalo, New York area close to the Niagara Falls.

By the summer of 2011, I had percepted the blue planet where the judgement seat and the throne of the Zion king resides this blue planet is located straight thru the burning sun and is located above the Zion center of our universe and is located right below of our heavenly father's heaven and all the men are awaiting in line for their own individual judgement day. And the throne of the king of our universe says as it is written: "Kotulookeekootetu."

And by the winter of 2011, I had a perception of the golden planet it is the children's planet and it is located to the upper left side of the blue planet and a bit lower than our heavenly father's heaven. And this golden planet is straight up and above the green vegetable planet. This golden planet is made out of solid gold. There is no food on this golden planet. This golden planet is full of children, and their shepperd is the king of Persia, King Mohammad Reza Shah Pahlavi, and the children keep playing and singing and dancing all day and all night until they all fall asleep on and around their shepperd.

By winter 2011, I perceived the other end of our expanded universe at the year 88888 light years away from the golden "Nero" end which is at the year of 99999. But at the other end of our expanded universe, at the year of 88888 there is a giant golden "Z" zenith which keeps on ringing zang, zing, zung zeng, zong. And no one nor anything can get close to it; because of the black pilot man and his black spaceship which looks like a giant condor vulture and when the black pilot starts his engine the black spaceship which has four winged "X" shaped module starts to drag its enormous eight chained bearded bottom, it is dragging its flaps as it picks up speed and it begins to travel faster and faster and these giant chains turn hot and they fume under the belly of the black pilot's spaceship and this vultured spaceship is invisible and it goes into a stealth mode and the black pilot and this spaceship's only objective is to capture and kill the king of Persia and drag king of Persia's body back to the "Z" zenith end of our universe at the year of 88888 light years away of our expanded universe.

By spring of 2011, I perceived that there is the red jungle planet of women and the animals and dinosaurs playing on the right side of our zioned center of our universe. It is located straight thru the moon and straight thru the burning sun and it is on the right side of the Zion center of our existence. The red jungle planet is where the women come from and at its bottom, there is a giant fish red drum fish which is scoping from right to left semi-circling, back and forth from left to right. And this giant red drum fish is also scoping the bottom horizon of the red planet semi-circling.

By spring of 2013, I had percepted the Zionist Zion kingdom at the center of our universe. It is a massive, enormous, collection of gray rotating from left side it arcs up from the spermicide, suicide, homicide, genecide, supercide and it reaches the Aryan king's skull and then it arcs down to the right side: super polymer, superchloride superfloride, supercyphone, supercycle. And the rotating, thick, gray base it is written: "Zion King." And then from below the thick disc base it hangs a strap of invisible, colorless, gray, silver snake "Mary" and it rotates behind as written: "Ghost Queen Vast &" (back to the rotating front): "Zion King."

There is an old notion that God sent just one person, a human a man on a flying horse with wings on to our dirt earth long long time ago named: "Pegasus." And this Pegasus landed in Persia and then our heavenly father's heavenly goddess followed this person on her white unicorn horse which is from the Zionist's kingdom and now that both Pegasus and unicorn horses have died and perished; this goddess has become our queen of vast universe by the spring of 2011 in Las Vegas, Nevada, USA. I had yet another perception that there is a dark black hollow cylinder passage on the upper right sector of the burning sun. But this cylinder is cold and cool enough for the superpolymer elastic plastic Celtic superpolymer arm which goes thru the cool cold dark hollow black cylinder in the upper right sector of our burning sun and this arm reaches all the way to the dirt earth in order to pick up and grab and teleport any human body and it teleports and retracts back up to the Zionist's kingdom in the center of our universe.

By spring of 2012, in Los Angeles California I had another perception that a singular hetrogenous, UFO, a giant sized motorized purple color machine type mechanized UFO, driven by the purple pilot who keeps on picking up one man at a time after another man at a time from the Mayan Aztec area and the purple pilot and the purple UFO keeps taking these men, one at a time and the pilot takes the humans to the blue planet, the judgement planet. And the purple UFO drops off the human men, one at a time back and forth from the dirt earth to the judgement blue planet. And once you get to the blue planet, you have to wait in line for your judgement day by the king of the universe. A human man gets to step off the blue planet onto the upper right side of the throne of the king of the universe and the human man gets to step onto one and then two yellow oriental homogenous UFOs floating and stepping into our heavenly father's heaven, and that is where our heavenly father resides with golden noisy angels bouncing on and off of him.

By the winter of 2016, I had another perception that there is a prison planet which is located above and beyond the children golden planet on the upper left side of our heavenly father's heaven and on this prison planet there is nothing but a set of seven bars of iron gate and a big giant golden dollar sign on the other end of the prison planet made out of solid gold and the only way any humans can get on this planet is by riding on the back of the big pig eating human bloody boar which keeps on passing gas back and forth from the prison planet to dirt earth.

By spring of 2016, I had a perception that a huge, giant enormous inverted upside down UFO pyramid in outer atmosphere of dirt earth suspended on top of Egypt. This pyramid UFO was awaiting to pick up and lift up one by one of more Hebrew human souls to complete its infrastructure made up of other Hebrew souls. It is not yet completely covered by Hebrew human souls. Part of the base of the corner of the UFO it is still made of Egyptian dirt earth. The entire pyramid UFO is covered by purple, black, royal blue, golden, white sparkling, burgendy colored souls of humans from dirt earth Egypt and it is sometimes sparkling like stars, except the corner base of the pyramid is still made out of dirt earth from Egypt.

By winter of 2017, I had more perceptions of 2 more UFOs which are white colored ring shaped flying from the upper right side of the blue planet just before any human man steps on to our heavenly father's heaven and these 2 UFOs land on top of the island of Japan, they get one on top of each other and become double white rings of UFOs by the same time of the winter of 2017, I also had another perception that a seperate UFO has landed on the islands of United Kingdom the Stonehenge and after the stones stood upright for this UFO's landing, there was a man present at the Stonehenge and as he eyewitness the UFO's landing the two UFO pilots: one royal blue and the other pilot was golden yellow pilots opened their windshield and once the two UFO pilots: the blue and the yellow pilots saw the human being, they instantly flew back up to outer space. And the stones moved back and fell into their original position by the beginning of 2016 winter around Christmas time, Princess Leila Shah Pahlavi had become a Liontess in outer space within the Zion kingdom. And then she was hungry and thirsty for food and water. And at the same time, Princess Leila Shah Pahlavi put her left hand on my right eye and scratched the right side of my face with her left four fingers, meaning that Princess Leila Shah Pahlavi was trying to tell me that her mother Queen of Persia will kill 4 of my ex-girlfriends. And then at the same time, Prince Ali-Reza Shah Pahlavi had become the Zion king as a lion. Prince Ali-Reza Shah Pahlavi put his left hand with one motion under my throat on the left side of my skull. And then the Pahlavi family dynasty told me in Farsi that "I have made them highly emotional in my writings bac on dirt earth." Then Princess Leila Shah Pahlavi ordered me not to say anything to her mother Queen of Persia that this is all a fiction and then one of my eyewitnesses Ms. Tigress Sushimi Motorola appeared in my face, as a Japanese white tiger in the middle of Zionist kingdom in the center of our universe. And then Princess

Leila Shah Pahlavi took me back to the center of the universe Zion kingdom, and then the Lioness Princess Leila Shah Pahlavi jumped on top of my head and she disappeared for exactly 24 hours. And then Princess Leila Shah Pahlavi appeared in my face and she said in Farsi very happily that "she has food for me and herself" at the same time Princess Leila Shah Pahlavi said again in Farsi in outer space in the middle of Zion kingdom "that she has lunch for both of us." And then Princess Leila Shah Pahlavi congradulated me and my new girl-friend during Christmas of 2016. And just before she said congradulations in Farsi Princess Leila Shah Pahlavi said "God bless you, Babak" in Farsi and by April 2018 calender year, King Mohammad Reza Shah Pahlavi King of Persia was piloting his golden hat spaceship in order to transport Princess Leila Shah Pahlavi, but Princess Leila Shah Pahlavi kept pushing her father's, King Mohammad Reza Shah Pahlavi's golden hat spaceship away with her left hand as Princess Leila Shah Pahlavi was holding on for dear life to Princess Ashraf Shah Pahlavi with her right hand at the bottom of the red jungle planet. And after a few days her Majesty Princess Leila Shah Pahlavi could not and she was not able to hold back her father's spaceship with her left hand. And then at exactly 2:04 AM (PST) on the date of August 15th, 2018: Princess Leila Shah Pahlavi and Princess Ashraf Shah Pahlavi were transported by the golden hat Pahlavi spaceship guided by King Mohammad Reza Shah Pahlavi to the golden "Nero" end of our universe.

By January 5th, 2019 A.D. the shepperd of the golden children planet King of Persia, King Mohammad Reza Shah Pahlavi is sound asleep and back on the golden planet of children and 40 seperate children have urinated all over the outer space of the golden planet and then their shepperd, King of Persia, started spacewalk from the children golden planet all the way around the bottom of the burning sun and King of Persia spacewalked all the way to the red jungle planet full of women and animals. And then King Mohammad Reza Shah Pahlavi, King of Persia, passed the dinosaur red drum giant fish at the bottom of the red planet, the jungle planet just like Jupiter full of women and full of dinosaurs animals. Because King of Persia is also King of the Jungle Red Planet. And on January 5th, 2019 I perceived all of the red planet's jungle movements of the animals and dinosaurs because King of Persia was present on the red Jungle Planet and he was looking for his queen vast inside the Jungle Red Planet.

The golden hatted UFO is made of gold on gold and only the King of Persia can fly it. This particular UFO has already went back and passed the dirt earth and the tumultuous space below dirt earth all the way back passed the black hole and the golden hat UFO has landed on the golden giant, saxophone enormous horn. The King of Persia was out of the giant red drum fish's eye scope range at the bottom of the red Jungle Planet. And then, the King of Persia was by the bottom of the shining solar sun area spacewalking towards the Children Golden Planet. By spring of 2019, January February March of 2019 I am having a perception of a tiny, small, metamorsel of a planet which is located well below of our Zionist's center of our universe. And on this planet there is a bunch of misfit UFOs playing their musical instruments for all the other planets in harmony. And the only other location that these misfit UFO's and their gadgets and musical instruments get together for a concert and play music in harmony is in the northern deserts of Shiraz in Iran, Persia. I saw them in person back in 1977.

By spring of 2019, I just had another perception that the giant enormous pyramid triangular UFO hanging upside down on top of Egypt flew away and vanished into outer space straight passed the Zionist center of our universe and up and over our heavenly father's heaven and it has landed over the horizon of another planet full of black people men, women and children. This purple planet is located on the upper right side of our heavenly father's heaven.

By spring of 2019, I had another perception that the Zion king is looking with his sonar rod prescope down towards dirt earth from our Zionists center of our universe straight down and bent at a 90° angle probed and ready and leveling to a needled point of a punctured spiritual being with a broken emotional status of despair and frustration and a defenseless human losing their soul.

By spring of 2019, I had another perception that there is a steel sturdy long bridge between the red Jungle Planet, the women planet, on the right side of our Zionists center of our universe and this bridge of shiny sturdy steel extend from the red planet to the blue planet, where the men get judgement passed on them by the king of the universe. The blue planet where all the mankind have to wait in line for judgement day by the king of the universe sitting on his silver, gray mercury throne. This bridge allows the women to travel back and forth to the blue planet on a big conductive attached UFO which is also made out of steel sturdy metallic mangenese. And the men from the blue planet's conductive silver steel sturdy mangenese UFO ship is Captain Zero's mothership which originally crashed into the dirt earth long time ago as it is written in my first book: titled "Space Walker."®

By spring 2019, I had a perception that the UFO which lands in the United Kingdom Stonehenge with the blueman and the yellow man pilots, that UFO travels from the blue planet judgement day planet to the golden planet of children; back and forth, the UFO travels and transports the children from the golden planet to the blue planet.

On 3/5/2019 at exactly 9:07 pm (PST) Princess Leila Shah Pahlavi was perceived by me, Mr. Babak Naderi to be free from the golden "Nero" end of our universe, at the year 99999 light years away and the "Allah" golden spaceship has landed her majesty on the red Jungle Planet. And at the same time the 40 small young children from the Children Golden Planet urinated into outer space off the golden planet. But the King of Persia their chapron of the 40 small, young children; the King of Persia is sleeping. While on the red Jungle Planet, the red drum giant fish is scanning and scoping and looking for the King of Persia to wake up on the golden children planet and the red drum fish is waiting for King of Persia to wake up and spacewalk over to the red Jungle Planet. And all of these perceptions and heavenly words of knowledge fell on top of my head thru a funnel of all the waste from all the humans from heaven, which is shaped like a human intestine funnel stretching all the way from heaven and it splashed and splattered on top of my head by the summer of 2018 in Santa Monica, Los Angeles, California, USA and there is a comparable automatic "Σ" shaped broom which instantly started to clean this giant intestine funnell back up to our heavenly father's heaven.

On 5/31/2019 I also envisioned that Prince Reza Shah Pahlavi II has handed his majestic, liquidized, electrized superdensed, honenized, sweet smelling rod which holds on to the golden children planet's bottom hemisphere and this majestic rod extends down from the golden planet all the way to the green planet full of green vegetables and then it nobs out; and Prince Reza Shah Pahlavi II has handed this majestic rod to Prince Cyrus Pahlavi.

January 1st, 2017 Los Angeles, California, I had another extra sensory perception that I was (modus/midus) golden man at the bottom of the Atlantic Ocean, the city beneath the queen in my room and I was shining as golden bright illuminating human in a complex of rooms which are built for any humans to be restored; one room on top of each other and the rooms were built out of steel, all the way down below the ocean shores of France and Italia and I was the only survivor, but that was 77777 years ago. And after I reached the land above this city in modern human history city of Alexandria, I had to walk all the way from Europa to the Arabia "where is Shadow?" and say it out loud and reach the Persian Gulf.

On 5/31/2019 I had another extra sensory perception that at exactly 8:45 pm (PST) that the giant green tree which was in Buffalo, New York has detached itself and went up and twisted and retracted back up to the green planet on the left side of the blue Judgement Planet; right passed the burning sun and passed the shining moon. And then it immediately retracted back towards our dirt earth on Saturday June 1st, 2019 all the way from the green planet straight down passed the burning sun and passed the moon and the giant, green tree has relocated and landed somewhere in the regions of New Delhi of Hindustan, India.

Back in 2017 summer time, June 21st 2017, I had a complete extra sensory perception of our expanded universe from one end to the other end. It is a misconception of our timely, scenery, energy, neroly widery. I am writing that I a human being in existence between the golden "Nero" end of the year 99999 in difference of the prison end of our year of 88888 and the difference is 11111 light years from each other of our far apart described and exampled and as it is written universe in my own writing above. That from our golden "Nero" end, we have to progress 5555.5 years before we reach our Milky Way Galaxy and at the current time and evening of after the death of Jesus Christ at the calender year of 2019.5 we have about another 3536 years to go before we reach and probe and penetrate the other galaxy "Andomedia," where the cumulated introvert middled plateau of 77777 years. And on the other end, beginning at the year 88888 and beyond the Heavenly Father's heaven and where the prison planet and the Erectusapian gianted enormous landed family UFO have as a complete family a man, a woman, a boy and a girl and the giant pyramid UFO, they have already for the next 7th generation traveled from that end of our universe and after 2222.2 years and a extra 5555.5 years. The black pilot of the vultured condor spaceship has probed and projected and penetrated 3333.3 years compared to only 2584.5 years of the golden "Nero" end. Do not get me wrong, there is 77777 years of humanity and life are in between the golden "Nero" end and the Erectusapian family big, black, pyramided UFO.

And on June 16th, 2019 I had another Extra Sensory Perception (ESP) by looking up at the solar sun at exactly 11:45 am (PST) about a perfect circumference also known as a (360°) degree circle. I believe it is because of my American Father Mr. William Dorrel and my Persian father Mr. Esfandiar Naderi have finally me each other in our Heavenly Father's Heaven. It is called "the circle of life" on our dirt earth planet.

June 18th, 2019 at the (±) ionized planet in a positivized crystalized, openized, emotionalized, diamonized eternalized stones of women, who wanted to merry their husbands. This planet is located straight from our dirt earth, straight passed the moon and straight passed the burning solar sun and passed the red Jungle Planet full of women and the dinosaur animals and under the superconductive bridge, where the UFO travels and transports the women from the red

Jungle Planet. And as it is written before this UFO superconductive train travels back and forth between the red Jungle Planet to the blue planet the Judgement Blue Planet on the left side of the red Jungle Planet. This crystalized, diamonized, eternalized planet full of arraying sparkling gems of stonized innocent souls of humanized angels from our dirt earth, who were women in love with their men from the dirt earth. This planet is located on the upper side of the superconductive train UFO and below the footsteps of the double ringed UFOs before any man can step on to our heavenly heaven.

Once upon the day of November 17th, 2019 his Imperial Highness (HIH) his majesty king of kings, King Mohammad Reza Shah Pahlavi has entered the beds of heaven along side with my Persian father Mr. Esfandiar Naderi and my American father Mr. William Dorrel. Ashes to ashes, dust to dust may they rest in peace from all of us.

THE END.

Printed in the United States
By Bookmasters